Daddy's Sandwich

This Faber book belongs to

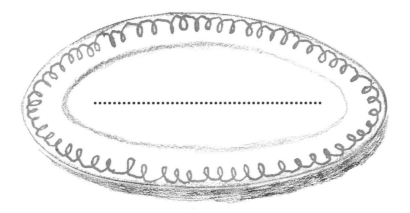

'I did like it a lot, it is very funny.'
Keira, age 3

'Let's read it again! Let's read it again!
Let's read it again!'
Alex, age 3

'Thank you to the lady who wrote it and whoever did the pictures. Now I am off to make a sandwich for my daddy. Mummy can you help me with the toaster?'
Daisy, age 5 and mum Joanna

'That book is CRAZY! That sandwich would taste disgusting! It was fun.'
Izzy, age 5

'She's so silly my face fell off.'
Dexter, age 3

'It was very funny. It made me think of what I would put into MY Daddy's sandwich and that was even funnier.'
Ibrahim, age 4

'I will make daddy a sandwich but I won't be in it as his cheese is tooooooo stinky.'
Joseph, age 3

'That was good. That's a big sandwich. Why didn't she put jam in it?'
Finley, age 4

'I like the kitty cat.'
Ellis, age 3

For darling Ruby,
the most quirky and
creative of little chefs X
P. J.

For my dad
L. H.

First published in the UK in 2015
by Faber and Faber Limited
Bloomsbury House,
74–77 Great Russell Street, London WC1B 3DA

Text copyright © Pip Jones, 2015
Illustration copyright © Laura Hughes, 2015
Design by Ness Wood

HB ISBN 978-0-571-31182-8
PB ISBN 978-0-571-31183-5

10 9 8 7 6 5 4 3 2 1

The moral rights of Pip Jones and Laura Hughes have been asserted.
A CIP record for this book is available from the British Library.

FSC
MIX
Paper from responsible sources
www.fsc.org FSC® C020056

→ A FABER PICTURE BOOK ←

Daddy's Sandwich

Written by
Pip Jones

Illustrated by
Laura Hughes

ff

FABER & FABER

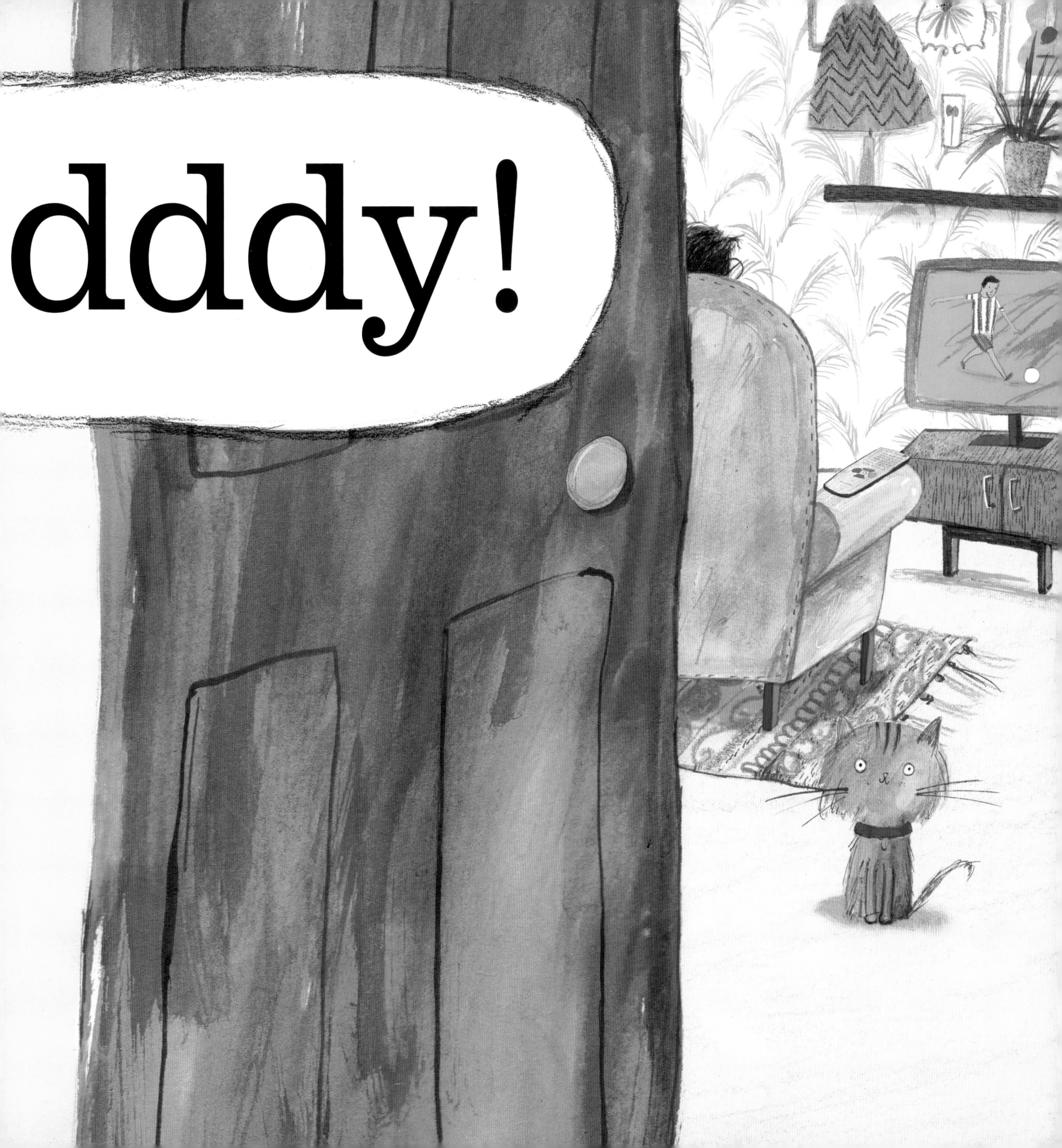
dddy!

'Daddy, would you
like a sandwich,
with all your
favourite things?'

'Mmm!
Yes please.'

Now, what does Daddy **really** like?

bread

Daddy loves
white bread,
crusty on the
outside.

Daddy loves butter,

but not **too** much.

Daddy loves cheese that's a **teeny** bit stinky.

Daddy loves tomato,

with the green
bit pulled off.

Daddy loves biscuits
dunked in tea.

Daddy loves
his slippers,
'cos they're old
and **very** cosy.

Daddy loves his newspaper, but **not** when it's been crinkled.

Daddy loves his phone, with the sound up **very** loud.

Daddy loves the TV, and all those **boring** sports shows.

Daddy loves his bike, but it's **far** too **big** . . .

Oh! These will do!

Daddy loves Mum's bubble bath,
he sits in there for ages.

Daddy loves his camera,
and I'm **not** supposed

to touch it . . .
but maybe

just

this

once.

Daddy loves his banjo.

And his toolbelt.

And his deckchair.

Daddy loves . . .

my jelly beans.

Hmm . . .

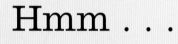

And my jigsaws!

My drawings!

My paddling pool!

My pop-up
books!

Daddy's sandwich
is nearly finished!

Just a **great big squirt**
of ketchup, and a slice of bread
to go on top.

But I think there's
something missing . . .

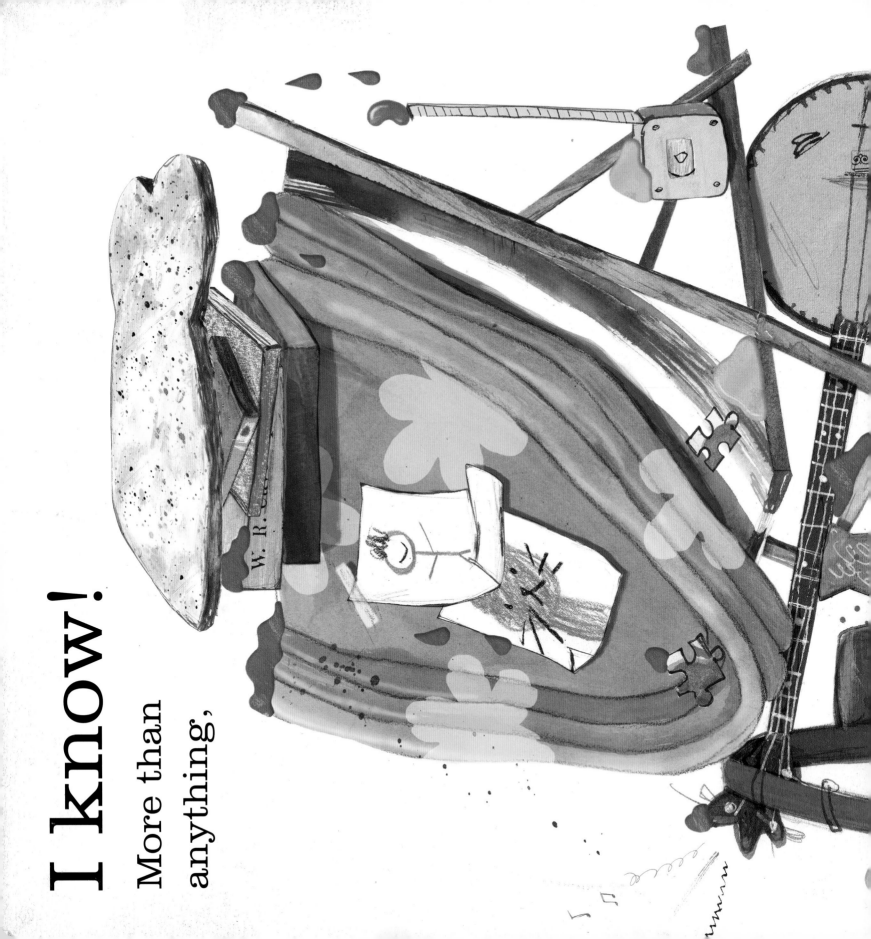

I know!

More than anything,

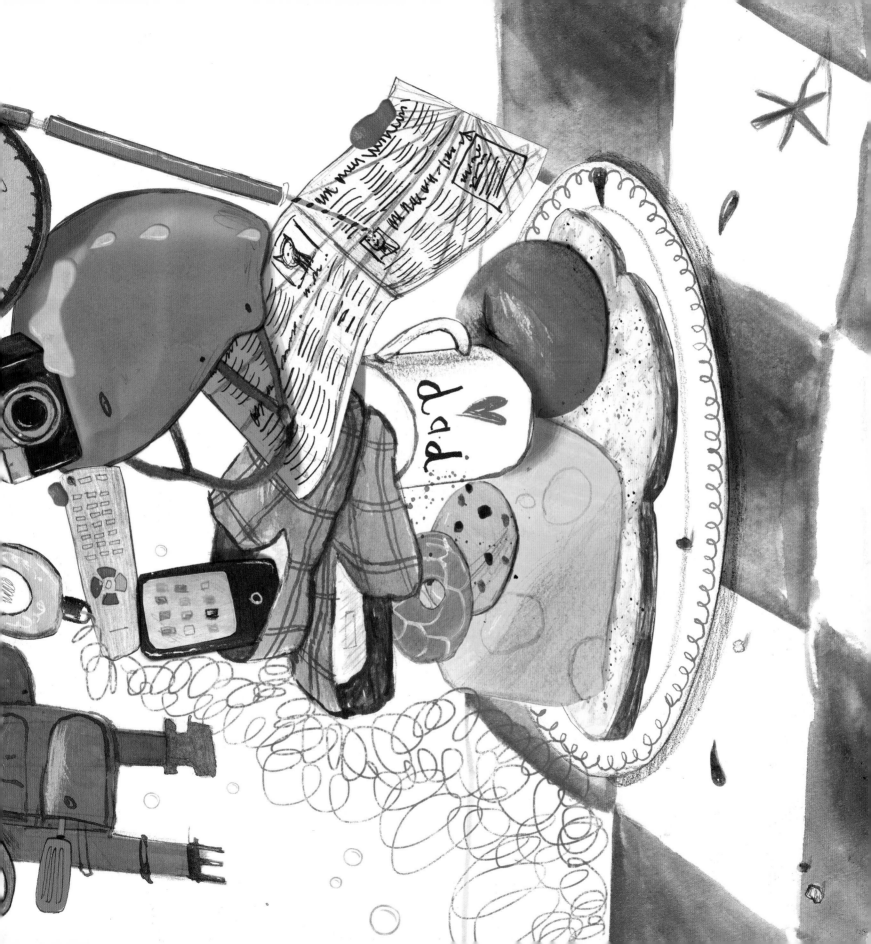

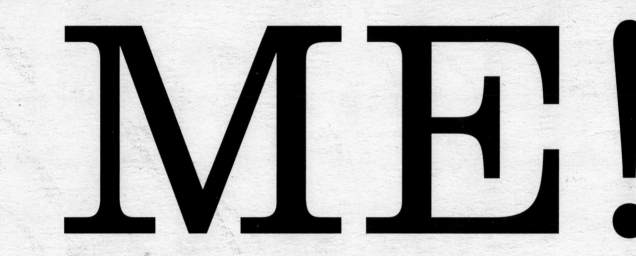

'DADDY!
Your sandwich
is ready!'